by Terry Collins   illustrated by Barry Goldberg

Simon Spotlight/Nickelodeon
New York London Toronto Sydney Singapore

Based on the TV series *The Adventures of Jimmy Neutron, Boy Genius*™ as seen on Nickelodeon®

 SIMON SPOTLIGHT
An imprint of Simon & Schuster Children's Publishing Division
1230 Avenue of the Americas, New York, NY 10020
Manufactured in the United States of America
First Edition 10 9 8 7 6 5 4 3 2 1
ISBN 0-689-85464-1

An eager Jimmy Neutron squirmed in his seat as Miss Fowl passed out the assignments. It was Science Report Day!

"Here are your subjects," Miss Fowl said as she handed the last folded sheet to Jimmy. "These are due in on Friday. Be creative!"

"Not a problem," Jimmy replied confidently, his mind already racing with scientific concepts far beyond the grasp of the average human mind.

Miss Fowl peered down at Jimmy from behind her glasses. "But not *too* creative," she said with a frown.

"Yeah, the last time brain boy got creative, he blew the roof off the chemistry lab," Cindy Vortex said, chiming in.

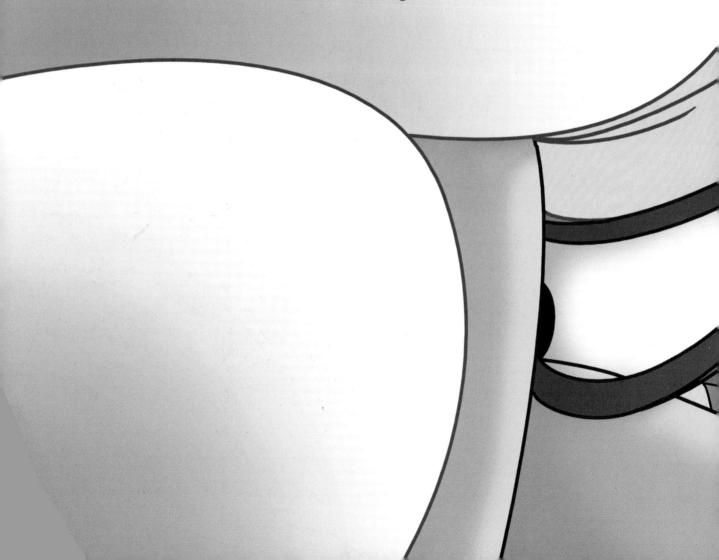

Jimmy opened his assignment. What would his topic be? Quasars of the Nebulon Galaxy Cluster? The art and commerce of static cling?

Felis catus was printed on the sheet in front of him.

"Felines? You mean cats?" he exclaimed in disbelief. "What is this? *First grade?*"

"You gotta trade with me, Cindy!" Jimmy pleaded as he trudged down the sidewalk on the way home from school. "All girls love cats. They're soft, and furry, and, um . . . do other cool stuff."

"Like cough up furballs. And use kitty litter—no thank you!" Cindy snorted. "This girl likes dogs!"

"What did you get, Carl?" Jimmy asked.

"The circulatory system! I already know lots about asthma," Carl said happily, puffing on his inhaler. "I can use the medical dictionary I got for my birthday!"

Later that day Jimmy entered his secret laboratory. His robot dog, Goddard, greeted him.

"Goddard, get ready to help me extract some information from the Internet!" Jimmy said as he linked the dog's access port to the lab's mainframe computer. "I want anything and everything relating to cats."

"While you're searching I'll grab a snack," Jimmy said, heading upstairs to the kitchen. "Back in a flash!"

Goddard's brain began flooding with trivia, facts, anatomy, and history of felines—from the common house cat to the saber-toothed tigers of long ago.

The robot dog sifted the data until it became too great to handle.

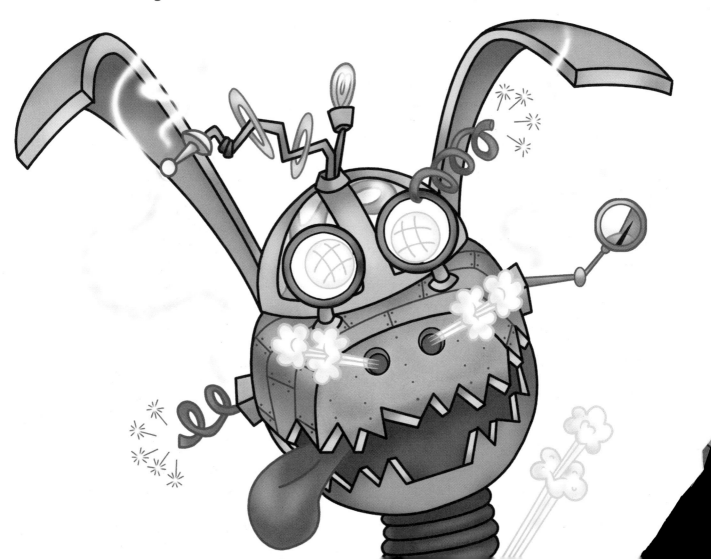

"Goddard! Bad dog!" said Jimmy as he returned to the lab. "You know you're supposed to stay off the equipment. Did you finish downloading everything for me?"

"*Meow*," purred Goddard. He then proceeded to use his tongue to clean his front leg!

Jimmy motioned for Goddard to join him at the computer screen, but instead he jumped to the floor and ran out the door!

TIGER

"Goddard! What's wrong with you?" asked a confused Jimmy as he chased after his disobedient pooch. "Keep this up and . . . no aluminum for supper!"

The canine promptly strolled away—tail and nose in the air.

"That's weird," Jimmy mused. "He's not acting like a dog. He's behaving like . . . a cat!"

"What are you talking about?" Cindy asked as she and her dog Humphrey walked over.

Humphrey gave Goddard a friendly sniff. Goddard yowled i[n] reply and ran for the nearest tree!

As Jimmy and Cindy looked on, Goddard hissed and spat at the barking dog below.

"This is totally weird, Neutron—even for you," Cindy said, backing away slowly with Humphrey. "Miss Fowl said not to be too creative, remember?"

"But, it's not my fault. . ." Jimmy protested.

Jimmy rescued Goddard and took him into the laboratory for a mental checkup. He examined data comparing Goddard's brain waves from a previous diagnostic to the current pattern.

"No way! You must have gotten a computer virus off one of those cat Web sites you accessed for my report," Jimmy said, moaning.

Goddard purred happily as he played with a ball of copper wiring.

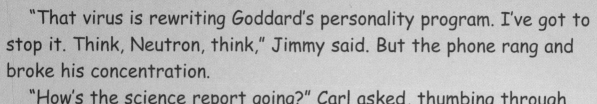

"That virus is rewriting Goddard's personality program. I've got to stop it. Think, Neutron, think," Jimmy said. But the phone rang and broke his concentration.

"How's the science report going?" Carl asked, thumbing through his medical dictionary.

"Cats aren't exactly the friendliest creatures on the planet," Jimmy said, watching Goddard use his chair as a scratching post.

"My mom used to have a kitty . . . but I'm allergic," Carl said. "She told me that to truly know a cat you've got to get inside its head."

"Get inside its head?" asked Jimmy, leaping into the air. "Carl, you're a genius!"

"I am? Goodie!" Carl said, beaming with delight.

"Carl, can you come over?" Jimmy asked. "I might need your help later."

"Sure," Carl said, standing up tall. "We can do some genius stuff together."

LLAMAS
IN THE MIST

MEDICAL
DICTIONARY

Working with materials scavenged from the kitchen and a pair of his dad's old sunglasses, Jimmy tried on his latest invention—a two-way virtual reality helmet!

"Okay, Goddard. I need to take a look inside your brain," Jimmy announced, plugging the helmet's access cord into the dog's data port.

"Make room! I'm swinging into your cerebellum!"

With a crackle of energy, the view before Jimmy's eyes faded from his laboratory . . . to a howling sandstorm.

"Gosh, no wonder Goddard's malfunctioning," Jimmy muttered. "The inside of his head is full of wind and sand."

The boy genius was baffled. What did the desert have to do with cats?

From far off, Jimmy heard a faint, yet familiar, bark.

"Goddard!" Jimmy called, following the faint barks. "Keep barking!"

But when Jimmy stepped over the last sand dune, he saw that Goddard's brain was infested with feline sights and sounds!

There was only one explanation: The computer virus he downloaded had somehow combined with the cat research!

"Now I get the Egyptian motif!" said Jimmy as he read stray bits of cat data painted on stone tablets. "Cats were originally desert animals. There wasn't any water around, so that's why they clean and groom themselves with their tongues. . . ."

"Brain blast!" Jimmy whispered as images of water, sand, cats, and dogs raced along the pathways of his mind, swirling together and creating a newly born idea.

Suddenly Jimmy realized what was missing from within Goddard's mental landscape.

"Here, kitty, kitty, kitty," Jimmy said as he unhooked the virtual reality helmet. "That's a good kitty cat."

"*Meow?*" purred Goddard as he took one step forward toward his owner.

"Thirsty, boy? Time for a cool refreshing drink!" Jimmy cried as he grabbed the confused canine and bolted for the exit.

"Well, here I am!" Carl announced as Jimmy ran into the Neutrons' backyard.

"Perfect timing! Turn on the water faucet!" Jimmy said as he grabbed the hose and directed the stream right into Goddard's face!

"*Meowww! Pftt!*" Goddard spat, sparks flying as the liquid splashed across his metal skin and circuitry.

"Jimmy! What have you done?" a horrified Carl asked.

"I gave my dog a brain wash!" Jimmy replied, leaning over the drenched Goddard. "Speak to me, boy!"

Goddard shook the water off his back, then gave Jimmy a lick. "*Bark!*"

"Goddard needed a jolt to his system, so I soaked his neuroreceptors," Jimmy explained. "Cats hate water, so I knew the shock would reboot his programming."

Carl gave Goddard a pat on the head, and then sneezed. "Are you *sure* he's back to normal?"

"Why do you ask?" said Jimmy.

"Ah-ah-choo!" Carl sneezed again. "I told you . . . I'm allergic to cats."